N

MAP

E

TO SUE, MICHAEL, AND THE BRIGHT 1993 AUGUST AT 'LA CASA DEL PINO'

MY MAP BOOK
COPYRIGHT © 1995 BY SARA FANELLI
FIRST PUBLISHED IN 1995 BY ABC, ALL BOOKS FOR CHILDREN,
A DIVISION OF THE ALL CHILDREN'S COMPANY, LTD.
33 MUSEUM STREET, LONDON WC1A 1LD, ENGLAND NOV 1 '95
PRINTED IN SINGAPORE. ALL RIGHTS RESERVED.

LIBRARY OF CONGRESS CATALOGING-IN-PUBLICATION DATA
FANELLI, SARA.
  MY MAP BOOK / BY SARA FANELLI.
    P.   CM.
  SUMMARY: A COLLECTION OF MAPS PROVIDES VIEWS OF THE OWNER'S
BEDROOM, SCHOOL, PLAYGROUND, AND OTHER REALMS FARTHER AWAY.
  ISBN 0-06-026455-1. — ISBN 0-06-026456-X (LIB. BDG.)
  [1. MAPS — FICTION.] I. TITLE.
PZ7.F2213 MY 1995   94-48834
[E] — DC 20   CIP
                                                AC

1 2 3 4 5 6 7 8 9 10
FIRST AMERICAN EDITION, 1995

SARA   FANELLI

MY
MAP

M   A   P

B   O   O   K

HarperCollins*Publishers*

MAP OF MY FAMILY

ME

MOMMY

+ MY DOG
BUBU

GRANDPA
+
GRANDMA

MY
SISTER

DADDY

COUSIN
LOUISE

COUSIN
PETER

COUSIN
GEORGE

AUNT
LUCY

UNCLE
MICHAEL

AUNT
ROSE

GRANDMA
+
GRANDPA

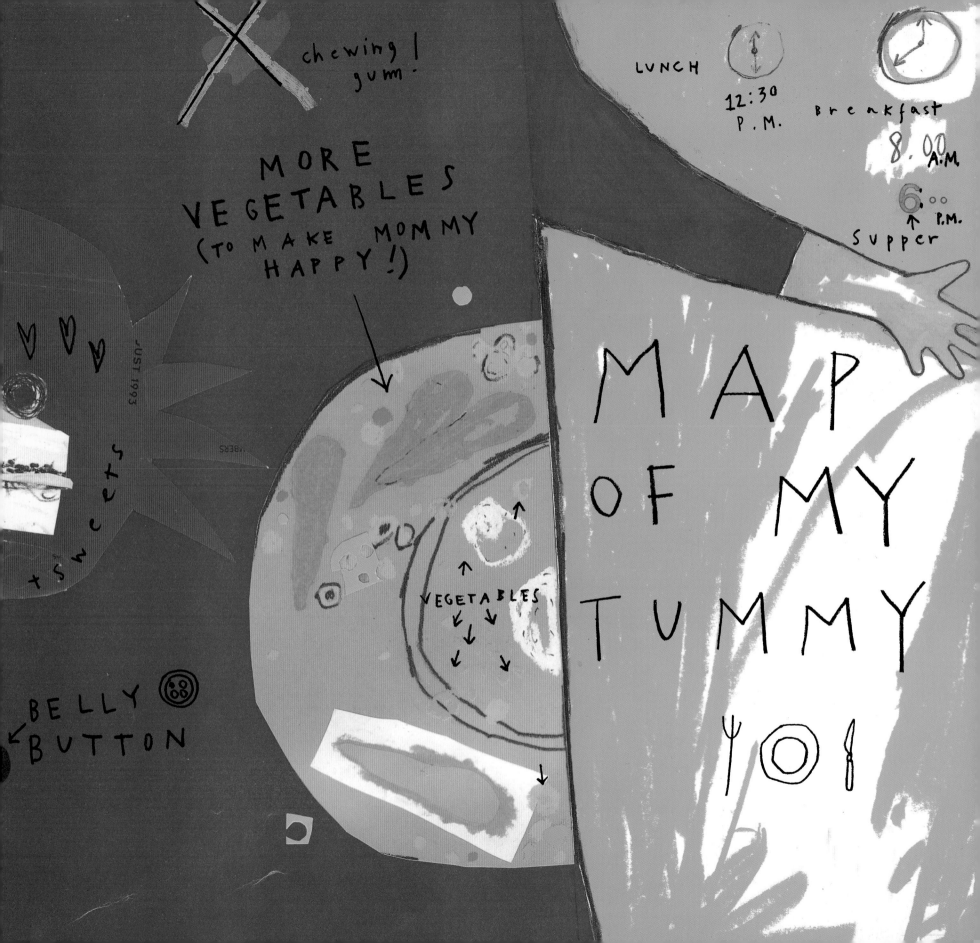

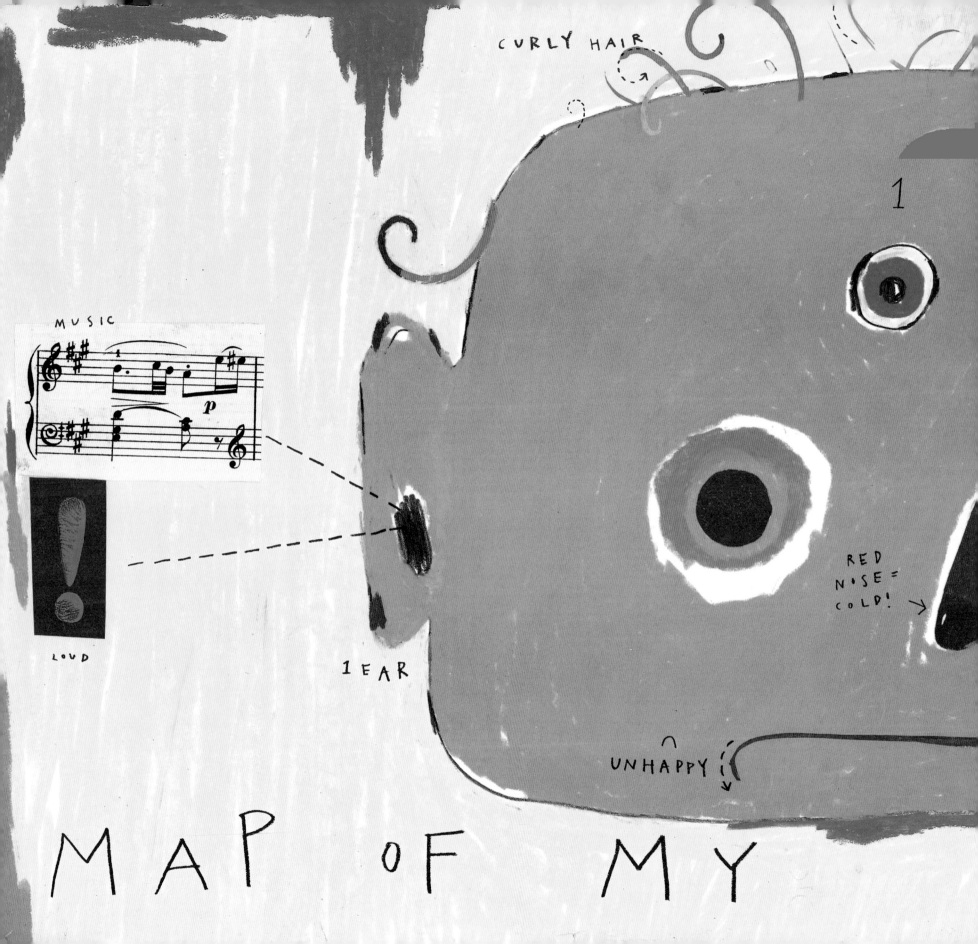

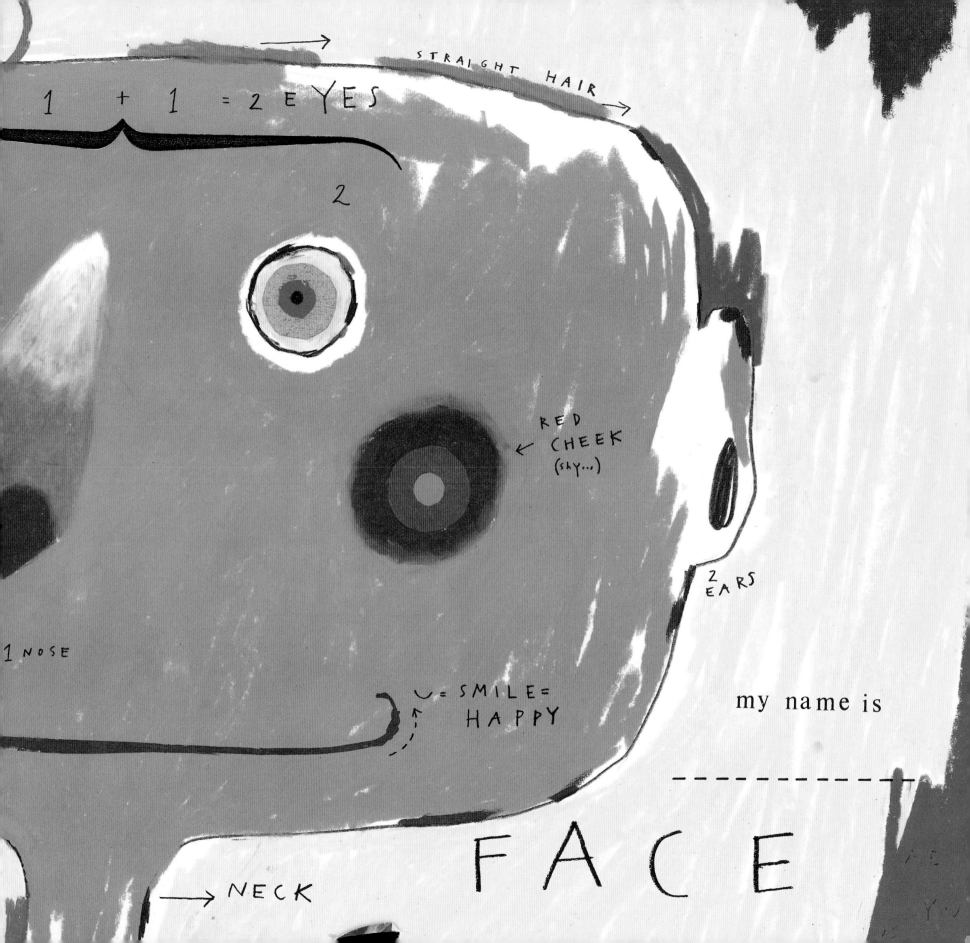

M A P S